GW00771440

This book is dedicated to my amazing nephew Noah Carter Larose.

Billy Be Kind was a kind little mouse.

He met Noah Carter one day at his house.

Little Noah was unhappy

and did not know what to do.

He'd lost his favorite truck,

'Old Boy Blue'.

He looked in the closet

and under his bed,

then took his blanket and covered his head.

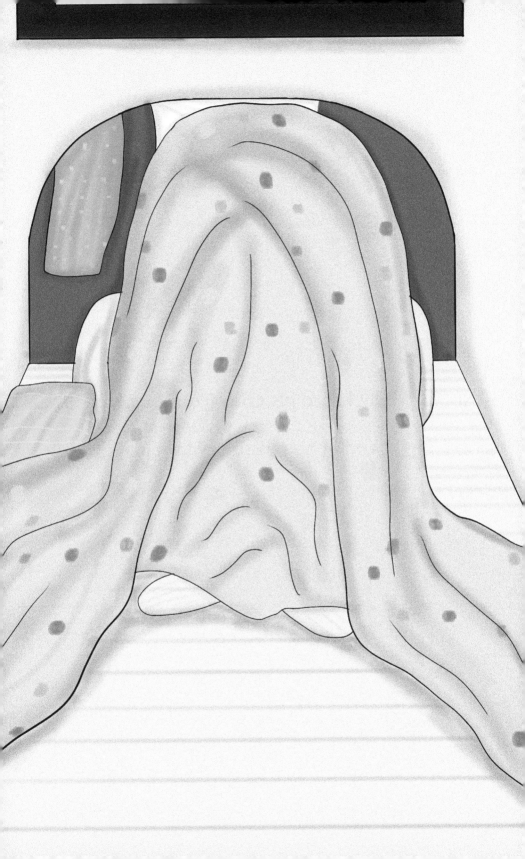

Billy heard his cries from far away

and in he ran to save the day.

"My blue truck, 'Old Boy Blue'

where could it be?

Could you find my truck for me?

Billy Be Kind knew just what to do.

"I will help to clean your room with you."

Noah looked upset

and he stomped the ground.

"I want my truck now and it can't be found!"

"The first step", said Billy,

"is to fix your bed

and put away your toys instead."

They filled the bins with lots of junk

and put his toys inside the trunk.

They wiped the crayons off the doors

and swept the garbage off the floors.

He hung his sweaters on the hooks

and stacked up all his favorite books.

With a twinkle in his eyes

and a smile on his face,

he saw that everything

was in its proper place.

Now things were clean

and Noah could see,

just where 'Old Boy Blue' could be.

Right in the corner, next to his shoe

is where he last played with 'Old Boy Blue'.

His favorite truck he found at last.

"Vroom-vroom," said Noah, "he's really fast".

"Thank you!" he shouted.

Then from that day,

Noah promised to always put his things away.

# The End

# About the author

Kim Adams is a wife, mother, and the author of the Billy Be Kind children's series. She fell in love with the art of storytelling at a very young age and has been inspired ever since. Kim hopes to simplify some of life's important lessons as well as strengthen social skills through her rhyming short stories. She has always taught her children to lead with kindness and hopes to help spread her message to every little boy and girl.

Edited by Vincent LaDuca

# Coloring time with Billy Be Kind

CPSIA information can be obtained
at www.ICGtesting.com
Printed in the USA
LVHW080031120122
708313LV00002BA/70

9 781087 858920

# BIGFOOT
## and the
# GOLD STAR KID

by Shelley Anne Richter

DOODLE AND PECK PUBLISHING
Yukon, Oklahoma

Doodle and Peck Publishing
413 Cedarburg Ct
Yukon, OK 73099
405.354.7422
www.doodleandpeck.com

ISBN979-8-9853351-0-1 $\left(\text{sc}\right)$

ISBN979-8-9853351-1-8 $\left(\text{hc}\right)$

Temporary cataloging topics:
Bigfoot, sasquatch, yeti, Gold Star status, military family, swamp, latchkey kid


Library of Congress Control Number: 2021951174

Dedicated to my friend, Salome Vaughn, whose grandson, Heistin, is a constant light of love and the inspiration for this book.

SHELLEY ANNE RICHTER

What exactly is a Gold Star family?

Gold Star status is given to the immediate family member(s) of a fallen soldier who died while serving in a time of conflict. The 28th President of the United States, Woodrow Wilson, is credited with coining Gold Star Mother in 1918.
Gold star families—spouses, children, parents, siblings or others whose loved one died in service to our nation—are a vital part of our country's military community and history.

This status is the United States of America's vow to "never forget."

Simple activities designed to help parents and/or caregivers participate in, and support, a child's literacy skills and educational goals:

Linking to Literacy

- **Easiest:** Read the story. If you find a word you are not familiar with, write it down. Then look it up in a dictionary, or Google it!

- **More Difficult:** Words are made up of syllables, each having one vowel sound. Find several words in chapter one that have two, three, or four syllables. A printable activity sheet is available at the website below.

- **Challenging:** Verbs can be active or passive. Find several active verbs where the subject is doing the action. Then find several passive, or being verbs, where the action is being done to the subject, or by someone (or thing) else.

*For free, printable resources, visit www.doodleandpeck.com, click on the Linking to Literacy tab.

1

Wanting to get my chores out of the way, I wheeled the trash can down the driveway to the curb. A pebble hit my arm.

"Pssst." My friend stepped out of the shadow of a nearby tree. "Heistin, where's your mother?"

"At work," I replied.

"Cool!" said Jax. "Let's hunt for frogs in the swamp."

"Nah, I got things to do. You can help if you want. Besides, the swamp is full of alligators."

Plopping into a lawn chair, Jax said, "Come on. You're twelve years old. Don't be such a coward."

I prickled. "That hurt." Suddenly, the whole backyard lit up with fireflies. "It's not even dark yet," I exclaimed.

Jax's eyes bulged. "Dude! My grandpa says when weird stuff happens, our planet is on its way out."

I gulped. "Swamptiles will rule the world."

Jax turned pale. "See ya, Heistin." In his hurry, a sneaker slipped off his foot. He kicked it up in the air like a soccer ball, grabbed it, and sprinted toward his house.

I cupped my hands to my mouth and yelled, "Now who's being a coward?"

When I heard a croaking sound coming from the swamp,

my inner voice calmed me. *It's not so bad being home alone after school. I'm only by myself a couple of hours. I can take care of myself. And Mom comes home right after she gets off work.*

Mom always leaves me a note on the refrigerator. Today's note said,

> "Don't forget to do your chores and don't open the door for anyone after six—including that friend of yours."

My next chore was to fix the front door. If it wasn't tugged just right, the latch wouldn't catch. Maybe it could wait until later.

I plopped into Mom's recliner with my favorite comic book. It's about zombies. Engrossed in the gory pictures, I heard a sound. Was that someone jiggling the front door knob? I jumped out of the chair and peeked out the window. Right outside the door stood a gruesome hulk with bloodshot eyes! His pungent scent burned my nostrils.

I stumbled from the window and ran to the telephone. I dialed Mom's work number, but it went to her answering machine. I quietly hung up the phone. Whatever was lurking outside, I didn't want it inside. I tiptoed to the door again and checked the latch. Weird! It didn't stick anymore.

I ran back to the phone. "Jax. Jax. Gotta call Jax!" I punched in his number and waited.

At the other end of the line I heard, "Hello."

"Jax, a freaking monster is in my backyard."

"Yeah, and it's your mother." Jax has a weird sense of humor.

"Are you my friend, or not?"

"Okay, okay. I'll get my grandpa and we'll come over."

As soon as they arrived, I hurried them into the house and Mr. Bennington began questioning me. "What'd the critter look like, Heistin?"

"An ugly giant with thick brown hair!"

Mr. Bennington rubbed his earlobe and drawled, "Well, there's a legend around these parts that Bigfoot lives among us."

He lowered his voice. "Hunters have been trying to catch the half-man, half-ape for more than a hundred years."

"Please, Mr. Bennington," I cried. "Call the hunters right now! Tell them I saw Bigfoot! They need to get him out of my yard. Fast!"

Jax snarled. "You're a Gold Star Kid, Heistin. Shoot him with a paintball and run."

Mr. Bennington shushed his grandson. "Don't poke fun, Jax. Being a Gold Star Kid is an honor *nobody* wants." Jax ducked his head. His grandfather continued talking. "Years ago, I heard a story how Bigfoot freed a soldier's ankle from a bear trap. That was the beginning of a close friendship between the two."

Hearing a key slide into the front door lock, I panicked. "Mom will be furious with me if she finds company here after six."

Taking the hint, Mr. Bennington and Jax scrambled out the back door just as Mom walked in. She hugged me. "I see you repaired the lock."

"But, Mom, I didn't."

She frowned. "Then who did?"

"Bigfoot," I whispered.

"Absolutely!" Mom laughed all the way to the kitchen.

My chin sagged onto my chest. When I was four-years-old, on the eve of one of Dad's deployments, he stooped down and gazed into my eyes. "I'll miss you, son. Will you miss me?"

Without thinking, I shouted, "Abaluby!"

Dad roared. "Good one, Heistin."

From that day forward, "Abaluby" was our special word each time he was deployed.

When I crawled into bed that night, I thought of Mr. Bennington. He was great, but having my own dad again would be greater. I burrowed under the covers, leaving just my eyes and nose showing. A shadow fell across my bed.

Yikes! Was that Bigfoot lurking outside my window? I dove under my covers and wondered why no one had ever found

Bigfoot. All I had to do was sit in a chair and read a comic book and he shows up at my place. I wonder why.

2

A humongous web filled with green caterpillar-like worms drooped from a tree branch in the backyard. I steadied myself on the ladder, jerked the nest down, and pitched it into a steel drum, glad to put that chore behind me. The backdoor slammed.

"Heistin, I'm off to work," Mom called. "Don't forget to paint ladybugs and butterflies on the garden stones." As she backed out of the driveway, she rolled down the window and hollered, "And don't talk to anyone, I mean ANYONE, after six o'clock." *Geesh! Mom probably wouldn't think Jax was so bad if she knew Bigfoot was prowling around.*

A shrill whistle blasted my eardrums. I turned to see my buddy step from behind a cypress tree. "We have two hours to shoot hoops, Heistin."

I snickered. "Jax, did you know my mother is thinking of adopting you?"

He snorted. "Why? So she can have two servants?"

I climbed down the ladder and opened the shed door. "Grab a paint brush. You can help me get my chores done faster. The paint's in here."

Jax gawked at the huge army locker standing in the corner. Then he grinned and said, "That's big enough for Bigfoot to hide in."

I glared at him, then grumbled, "Come on, we're burning daylight."

I wanted to tell Jax about Bigfoot lurking outside my bedroom window, but I knew he probably wouldn't believe me. And Jax was wrong. Bigfoot was way too big to fit inside the footlocker. But the tack room in the barn? That was a different story.

An hour later, painting ladybugs and butterflies on the garden stones, Jax ran his tongue across his lips and said, "I'm thirsty. Let's take a break."

We headed for the kitchen and I grabbed two sodas out of the fridge. "I think we're making pretty good time," I said. "Thanks for helping me out."

Jax grinned. "Wait until you get my bill."

As we returned to our task in the backyard, a truck pulled into the driveway and Mr. Bennington climbed out. Jax motioned to his grandpa. "Take a look at what we've been doing."

Mr. Bennington studied each piece of our artwork. He ambled from where we had started behind the house to the final butterfly by the shed door. "You boys painted these?"

Jax puffed out his chest so far I thought his shirt might split. "Yep, Grandpa, we did."

Mr. Bennington nudged one with the toe of his boot. "What's this?"

"A butterfly," I said.

He walked back across the yard and toed another one. "What's this one?"

"That's a soldier's medal. Like the one Heistin has framed in his bedroom."

"Oh," Mr. Bennington said. "You boys did a good job considering you're using flat brushes instead of round ones." Suddenly an owl hooted, birds chirped, and something rustled out in the woods. Mr. Bennington turned to face the swamp. "Something's stirring up the wildlife out there."

"Maybe its Bigfoot," said Jax.

I frowned.

"Don't go scaring Heistin now. He's already got the heebie-jeebies about that man-ape roaming around his backyard." The old man gasped and pointed. "Boys, isn't that a baby owl trapped in that tree?"

Sure enough, a baby owl was stuck inside one of the wormy, webby cocoons. Wanting to free it, I grabbed a broom and lightly nudged the webworm nest. Jax stood on his toes, reached up, and carefully removed the owl from the web. "Poor thing, it hardly has any feathers. Should we take it to the vet, Grandpa?"

"I fear it's too far gone," he said sadly. "Best let nature take its course."

"He's shivering," said Jax. He shrugged out of his shirt and wrapped the baby owl in it.

I took the bird from his hands. "I'll take care of him."

"Grandpa and I will put the paint back in the shed and lock it up, Heistin."

"Thanks," I said, and headed toward the house. Inside my bedroom, I knelt on the floor and placed the owl on my bed. He had exactly five feathers on his tiny chest. His eyes were a bright yellow. I was glad he didn't try to scratch me with his claws. Watching the owl snuggle deeper into Jax's shirt reminded me of a picture of Dad holding an Iraqi child wrapped in his camo jacket.

Tap, tap, tap. Someone was tapping at the window. I stood and opened the blinds. Bigfoot yodeled. I blacked out.

## 3

I woke up dizzy, and wondering what had happened. Then I remembered Bigfoot had shown up again. Maybe he likes me, I thought. Maybe he's just lost. I yawned and fell into a deep sleep.

The next morning, as I trimmed vines in the backyard, Mom called, "Heistin! Heistin! Where are you?"

"In the backyard," I shouted back.

"I'm leaving for work now, dear. Don't forget to fill the birdfeeder. And don't open the door for anyone after six."

"And that includes that friend of yours," I mumbled.

"And that includes that friend of yours," echoed Mom.

I stowed away the garden shears, mixed sugar in a bottle of water, and filled the hummingbird feeder. The baby owl we had rescued needed to be fed again soon. I knew he would prefer a frog or a fish, but he would eat worms and crayfish. I hoped Jax would show up so he could help me with it. Jax had learned so much from Mr. Bennington about survival in the swamp. That knowledge would come in handy right about now.

That evening after dinner, Mom sat down to pay bills, so I snuck out to the barn. I knew she wouldn't approve of Hooty, so I had fixed a hiding spot for my feathered friend. I found an old jar lid, filled it with water, and placed it next to the tiny owlet. I hoped Mom would think my super-dirty jeans were from doing yard work when they were actually caked in mud from digging up worms.

Suddenly, I heard something that sounded like an air horn. When I reached the driveway, Jax hopped off a spiffy bike, and set the kickstand. I admired the bike's wire basket and oversized wheels. "Cool, dude! Where'd you get that?"

Jax blasted the horn again. "It used to be Grandpa's."

"You gotta be kidding me," I said.

"Nope. It's mine now."

"Can I hitch a ride?" I asked.

Jax grinned. "Climb on!"

I straddled the bike seat, pulled down my cap, and Jax took off. As we coasted down the steep two-lane road past the school the wind rushed past my face. Jax slowed to a stop and looked both ways before crossing the railroad tracks. Then, building momentum, he pedaled like a professional cyclist. Once we reached level ground, he turned the bike around, huffing and puffing, and started back up the hill to my driveway.

I slapped Jax on the shoulder. "How cool was that?" An owl hooted nearby. "Uh, oh. I almost forgot. The baby owl is hungry."

Jax's face clouded. "I may be wrong, but I think that was his mama we just heard."

We sprinted into the barn. But the baby owl was not in the stall where I had left it. I panicked. "Hope Bigfoot didn't get it."

Hoot, hoot. My eyes scanned the rafters. "Look, Jax! The mama owl and baby owl are both up there, side by side."

Jax shook his head. "Well, I'll be. Grandpa was right. We had to let nature take its course." He glanced at his watch. "It's getting late, Heistin. I've got to get going." He jumped on his bike and pedaled toward his house.

Later, in my bedroom, I fell backwards against my pillow. Thinking about the owl, I drifted to sleep.

14

I woke to Mom saying, "Your chore list must have tuckered you out. Bet you're hungry."

I rolled out of bed. "I'm starving!"

She walked toward the door, and then stopped. She picked up Jax's shirt off the dresser. "Whose shirt is this? It isn't yours."

"Uh, hmmm, what do you mean, Mom?"

"I do your laundry. I know it's not yours."

I stammered. "Oh, uh ..."

She shook it out and a feather floated to the floor. I leaned over to pick it up, but Mom beat me to it. I braced myself for a stern lecture. Instead, Mom grinned. "I want you to stick this feather in your cap, Heistin."

I gawked at her, wide-eyed. "Wh-what?"

Mom laid the shirt on the dresser. "I don't tell you enough how helpful you are to me when you do your chores without complaining." She turned on her heel. "Do you want thin crust or thick crust?"

After we ordered the pizza, I gazed across the room at a trophy I had won in the same basketball division as Jax. "Mom ..." I hesitated. "Why don't you like Jax?"

She pursed her lips, then picked her words carefully. "Do you know the difference between you and Jax?"

I shook my head no.

"You take after your father, Heistin. You're a hard worker and sensible. Jax is the opposite. He's lazy and takes unnecessary risks."

"He helped me paint the garden stones," I said. "And when we went bike riding he stopped at the railroad tracks."

The doorbell rang.

Mom jumped up and grabbed her wallet. "Dinner's here."

While we ate pizza and watched an old movie, I thought

about the baby owl, and Bigfoot. One was gentle, the other was … was … I really didn't know. If Bigfoot wanted to hurt me he probably would have by now.

But why was he hanging around?

4

The next afternoon, I found the usual note from Mom. It read: *Don't forget to tidy up the barn.* A knot quickly formed in my stomach. Bigfoot might be hiding in the tack room. There's safety in numbers, I thought, and then dialed Jax.

After ten rings, I hung up.

Outside, I took a deep breath and marched across the yard like a soldier in a parade. Inside the barn, I picked up a stiff broom and started knocking down cobwebs. Then I swept dried leaves and dirt from the track of the sliding door. *Wish Dad were still alive. Bigfoot wouldn't mess with him.*

Cre-eak. I stopped and gazed into the shadowy corners of the barn. The door of the tack room slowly inched open. Two hooded, bloodshot eyes peered out at me. I couldn't move. My body felt like cold, hard rock.

Bigfoot stepped out of the tack room. His fingernails were long and sharp. Then he rubbed his belly and screeched, "Aggghhhh!" Was he hungry? Hungry enough to eat me? I needed to get him some food and fast! Otherwise he'd be picking his teeth with my bones.

I ran as fast as I could to the kitchen. In the refrigerator I found a package of frozen chicken and a baggie of leftover pizza. I grabbed the pizza and ran back to the barn. Bigfoot whirled around, webs clinging to the fur around his mouth. "Yuck! Have you been eating those nasty webworms?" I slowly opened the baggy containing cold pizza. He rubbed his massive forehead, probably wondering if I was trying to trick him. Then he shuffled over, stuck his nose into the baggie, and took a deep whiff. With more bravery than I felt, I handed him three slices of pizza. He devoured them in one bite then licked tomato sauce from his beefy fingers. Slowly he closed his hand and held his fist six inches from my chest. I was scared, until I realized he wanted a knuckle bump. We bumped knuckles.

"Are you thirsty after eating all that food?"

Bigfoot bobbed his head. I grabbed a bucket and filled it with water. He bent down, picked up the bucket, and in one gulp drank it all.

A loud air horn squawked outside. Bigfoot yanked me closer to him. My nose stung, and my eyes watered like the first time I passed the elephant exhibit at the zoo. His matted fur felt like an SOS pad. Then he loosened his grip, grunted, and stepped further into the barn. Not knowing what to expect, I followed at a safe distance. We didn't make a sound. Even though Bigfoot was four times as wide as me, I succeeded in pushing him into the tack room.

Just as I slammed the door, Jax barged in. "Got any chores to do, Heistin?"

"You bet! I'm tired of garden stones with girlie butterflies and ladybugs." I pumped my fist. "Let's paint the barn like an American flag!"

"Cool!" said Jax. "I'll grab the red and white paint. You grab the blue." I swallowed hard. Bigfoot is in the tack room, and we're going to paint the barn? In what universe does this make sense? Jax clapped his hands like a circus clown. "Come on! We're burning daylight."

Two hours later, we painted the final star on Old Glory. "They're having the best of John Wayne's war movies tomorrow night at the Idol Theatre. You wanna go with me and Grandpa?"

"I'll have to ask my mom."

"Oh," he said glumly. "Her."

I winced.

It was as if Jax could see my pain. "I didn't mean it like that, Heistin. Your mom, well, your mom," he shrugged, "is your mom. What can I say?"

I gripped his shoulders. "My mom is a Gold Star wife and I'm a Gold Star kid. Can't you wrap your mind around how hard it's been for us since losing my Dad? War changed everything. Can't you understand that?"

Jax sniffed. "I won't ever bring up your mom again. Promise."

I gave him a sheepish grin. "Like John Wayne said, 'A man deserves a second chance. But keep an eye on him.'"

When Jax left a few minutes later, I stood before our artwork adorning the faded gray wood. I gave it a quick salute.

Snap! Whirling around I saw Bigfoot. He snapped his fingers, wiggled his shoulders, and mouthed the word, "PIZZA!!!"

I stammered. "I-I-I think Mom put some chicken out to thaw. I'll be right back." His bottomless pit eyes made my stomach lurch. I bolted toward the house, threw open the screen door, and scrambled into the kitchen. Pulling open the refrigerator door, I grabbed the package of chicken. Oh man! It's only six scrawny wings. I hustled back to the barn. But Bigfoot wasn't there. I searched the corral and the henhouse, but no Bigfoot. I fell to my knees out of breath.

Just then, Mom pulled into the driveway. She was an hour early. When she got out of the car, I could tell she'd been crying. I hurried over to her. "What's wrong?"

She held up the pink slip. "I got fired tonight. The company is downsizing." She gave me an odd look. "What are you doing with that package of chicken?"

I slowly raised and lowered my shoulders. "Thought tonight would be a good time to grill it?"

She sighed. "I'm in the mood for leftover pizza."

"We have brownies," I replied in a timid voice.

She leaned her chin on top of my head. "Sounds divine." She sniffled. "We may have to move, darling."

My stomach bubbled and fizzed like carbonated water. "Jax is a brat, Mom, but I love him like a brother. It will be too hard to say goodbye."

"Don't do this, Heistin," Mom cried. "I'm fresh out of ideas." Entering the house, she turned to flip on the porch light. With a spark and a sputter, the bulb blew out. "Oh, Heistin. I know it sounds silly, but that light made me feel safe." A few minutes later, I took the brownies and a glass of milk to Mom, but she had fallen asleep in her chair.

I stepped outside and breathed in the scent of swamp animals. Bigfoot was probably out there eating mosquitoes and webworms. With Mom out of work, I wouldn't be able to sneak him any more food. Since school was out for the summer, maybe I could get a paper route to help out. I gazed up at the stars. Now would not be a good time to ask Mom if I could go to the movies.

Suddenly, I felt like someone was watching me. In the moonlight, I saw Bigfoot standing in the shadows. I wondered if Dad was the soldier Bigfoot befriended? According to Mr Bennington's story, Bigfoot freed a soldier's foot from a trap. A memory bubbled to the surface of my brain. There was a time when Dad walked with a limp. How many more clues did I need? Then I noticed something really eerie. The porch light was on and glowing brightly.

Bigfoot grunted and disappeared into the darkness.

# 5

"Mom, I can do it," I yelled. "I'm twelve years old!"

"Heistin, power washing is a man's job."

"Please, let me try. If I can't handle it, I'll quit."

"We don't have any insurance now. What if you got hurt?"

"Look at my muscles, Mom."

She squeezed my biceps. "Maybe you are strong enough." She blew me a kiss and said, "Get out of here."

"Yes!" I shouted, and started for the door before she could change her mind.

"Heistin, if you want, we can barbecue that chicken on the grill tomorrow. Invite that friend of yours. Let's make it around one o'clock."

"Gee, thanks, Mom."

She swiped at her tears. "It'll be like a going away party."

All of a sudden I felt glum. I shuffled to the shed and hauled out the power washer. I faced the aluminum siding on the house, pointed the wand, and squeezed the trigger. The force of the water jetting out knocked me down.

"Let me do that, son."

Sitting up, I saw a stocky, average looking guy, dressed in camo. A bloodhound with very long ears lumbered at his side. "Who are you?" I asked.

The man squatted by his dog. "I'm Donnie Gibson. I work at the local Army Recruiting office downtown." He petted the dog. "And this is Gracie."

"You a hunter?" I asked.

Donnie reached down, gripped my hand, and pulled me to my feet. "Kinda sorta. Ever hear of Sasquatch?"

"No..."

"Some people call him Bigfoot." My heart jumped like a spooked mouse. Donnie patted his vest pocket. "With my digital camera, and Gracie's help, I'm going to prove Sasquatch exists."

Suddenly I felt uncomfortable. "It's been nice meeting you. But I need to get back to work."

"Not with this nozzle," the man said. "This one's built for high pressure. A different nozzle will be easier for you to handle. You have one?"

"I'll go look." I walked over to the shed and opened the door. To my horror, Bigfoot was crammed inside the army locker. I kicked the door shut.

Gracie began to bay. Thankfully the hunter had picked up the nozzle and was power washing the house. "Call me Donnie if you want," he yelled over the blast of water. "What's your name?"

"Heistin."

Donnie's eyebrows furrowed. "Huh?"

I felt a hand grip my shoulder. I whirled around. It was only Jax. He laughed, and offered me an apple. "Who's your new friend?" he asked.

I grumbled. "He's not my friend."

"Then what's he doing here?"

I shrugged. "He's a soldier at the armory. He seems nice enough. It's too soon to call him friend, though."

Gracie had wandered to the shed and was baying. Loudly.

Jax gulped the last of his apple. "Grandpa said bloodhounds only bay when they have something trapped." He tossed aside what was left of his apple and crept toward the shed.

22

I hollered, "Stop!" Jax turned around. I walked toward him like a zombie, and droned, "Bigfoot is in the army locker." Jax fell to the ground laughing. I tried to change the subject. "Hey, Jax. Guess what? Mom wants you to come to our cookout tomorrow at one o'clock."

Jax jumped to his feet. "Really? What about Grandpa?"

"Bring him, too."

Donnie called out, "Find another nozzle yet?"

I shook my head and wandered back to the power washer. "I'd like to try again if you don't mind."

"Not at all," Donnie said. "I have a suggestion, though. Plant your feet and brace your legs."

Channeling the strength of Iron Man, I pointed the nozzle at the house and squeezed the trigger. This time it didn't knock me over.

Donnie started walking backwards. "Good job! I like your determination."

Impulsively, I asked. "Gotta minute? I wanna show you something."

"Sure."

I turned off the power washer and he followed me to the barn. His eyes gravitated toward the flag. He touched it then jerked back his hand. "Paint's still wet. Who did this, anyway?"

"Me and my buddy. His grandpa was an Army Ranger."

"That makes it even more special." Donnie pulled his digital camera out of his pocket and snapped a picture. "Not many kids your age know what the stars and stripes stand for anymore." He touched the dog tags dangling from his neck.

Without thinking, I asked, "Want to come to our cookout tomorrow? It's at one o'clock?"

Donnie hesitated. "I appreciate the invite, but don't you think you should ask a grown-up first?" I scowled. He flinched then grinned. "You know, I would like to come to your cookout. Can I bring anything?"

"How about a pound of hamburger?" I asked.

"Absolutely."

Warm prickles crept up the back of my neck. I had almost blurted out "abaluby". It made me miss Dad more than ever.

"See you tomorrow." Donnie and Gracie made their way into the swamp and dropped out of sight.

I scuttled to the shed. Bigfoot was wedged inside without an inch to spare. "What are you doing?" I shouted. "There are hunters everywhere." I pulled and tugged to get his big frame through the open door, but it was useless. Finally he punched his way out through the roof.

"Hide! Bigfoot, hide!" I shrieked.

He disappeared quietly.

20

**6**

The next afternoon, Mom said, "The yard looks beautiful, Heistin. Your father would have been proud." She hugged me extra hard.

Just then, Mr. Bennington's car pulled into the driveway. Jax rolled down the window and said, "Hello."

"Welcome!" Mom called out with a smile.

"Grandpa, over here," Jax said with eagerness. "I want to show you this weird plant in the swamp." As they headed down the hill, an ATV roared into the driveway. Donnie cut the engine and climbed off. We bumped knuckles.

"Mom, meet Donnie Gibson. He works at the Army Recruiting office downtown."

Donnie reached out to shake Mom's hand and their eyes locked. "Aren't you Nora Chapman?"

Her voice barely audible, Mom said, "You went through basic training with Robert, didn't you?"

Donnie thumped his forehead and stared at me with a new awareness. "A dozen or so years ago, your husband wrote to me that you were expecting a baby boy and you planned to name him Heistin."

What? My dad had known Donnie? Crazy!

Donnie's eyes scanned the backyard. "And look at this place. All Robert ever talked about was finding a property with a lot of trees and space. This is definitely what he envisioned."

Reality reared its head. I moaned, "Wish we didn't have to move."

Donnie looked horrified. "Whoa! Why would you ever want to leave here?"

Mom frowned. "I lost my job. We have to. Quickly."

"Not if I can help it," said Donnie.

Mom's voice trembled. "What do you mean?"

"I only work part-time as a recruiter." Donnie grinned. "I'm also the chief executive officer of a nationwide janitorial service. And guess what, Nora? We need a local office manager. Come fill out the paperwork and the job is yours."

Mom's stunned expression slowly transformed into a beautiful smile. Her laughter trilled like music. "Thank you, Donnie. I'll be there first thing tomorrow!"

Recovering from my shock, I whooped, "All right!"

Donnie and I high-fived. He held out a package of hamburger meat and winked. "Robert taught me how to make 'cow patties' taste just like steak." Mom took the package and headed toward the grill.

Mr. Bennington and Jax returned from the swamp and slumped into a couple of lawn chairs. "Where have you been?" I asked Jax.

Mr. Bennington cleaned his eyeglasses on his shirttail. "Jax wanted to show me an odd plant in the swamp, but we spotted some giant footprints. We followed them, but they disappeared in the underbrush."

Uh, oh. My chest felt like it was being squeezed in a vise grip. I glanced over at Donnie. Fortunately, he was standing at the grill talking to Mom.

"Nora, didn't Robert tell me you played the clarinet in college?"

"The flute."

"My favorite instrument."

"No, your favorite instrument was the bugle."

"Shucks," Donnie snorted. "Robert didn't know when to be quiet."

"I play the harmonica," Jax blurted.

"That's an unusual instrument in this day and age," said Mom. "Can you play Old Susannah, for us, Jax?"

"No, but I can play "You Are My Sunshine." He took a harmonica out of his pocket and placed it to his mouth. As my friend moved the mouthpiece across his lips, the shrill notes stung my ears. Mom clutched her sides and doubled over, laughing.

Jax's face turned beet red.

After downing my second Donnie Burger, I excused myself and mustered the courage to enter the swamp alone. I sidestepped twisted tree trunks gleaming with moisture. Scummy water was puddled everywhere I looked. I flicked a beetle off my arm. When I found Bigfoot he was sitting on a stump with his chin resting in his giant hands. Relief washed over me.

I ran up to him. "Bigfoot, you live here? It's wet, and creepy, and downright depressing."

Bigfoot glanced up, plucked a low-flying bat out of the air, and cupped it in his huge hands. He nestled it against his cheek. Then he let it fly away. The big guy grunted and motioned for me to follow him. Rubbing my forehead, I decided to trust him.

We forged ahead further into the swamp. All at once, Bigfoot stopped, put his hands under my arms, and lifted me up to the crook of a tree. I had ridden a grain elevator once, and the sensation felt the same. In the tree was a nest with two baby owls. They must have thought I was their mama, because they opened their curved beaks and started making weird noises.

Bigfoot gently lowered me to the ground and gazed into my eyes. I knew what he was trying to tell me. The swamp was his home. I was his guest. Venturing further into the marsh, a fine mist embraced us, like the cool breath from a cascading waterfall. I glimpsed coiled snakes and slithery lizards. I couldn't imagine actually finding any place to sleep not teeming with serpents. I jumped when an alligator came out of nowhere and snapped its jaws at me. Bigfoot growled low at the gator and its short legs chugged to get away.

Warm rays of sunshine streaked down through leafy green trees. I felt Bigfoot touch the U.S. Army watch on my arm. I glanced at it and yelped, "Oh no! I've been in the swamp for almost an hour! Mom will be worried."

The creature Donnie called Sasquatch took my hand and started walking. For a moment, I thought we were lost. But my faith in Bigfoot was rewarded. In the distance, I could see my house. Donnie and Mom were calling, "Heistin! Heistin! Where are you?"

We could see the flashing lights of a county sheriff's car as it pulled into the driveway. Jax was pleading with the deputy and pointing toward the swamp.

Donnie had climbed on his ATV and started the motor. He yelled to Mom, "I'm going to get Gracie. She'll find Heistin."

Mr. Bennington flailed his arms and pointed to the helicopter hovering in the sky. "Keep an eye out for Bigfoot."

Digging into my pants pocket, I pulled out the digital camera, I had borrowed from Donnie. As the search party drew closer, I gasped, "Need a really fast favor, Bigfoot."

He stood to his full height and nodded. I held up the camera and snapped his picture. Then, my friend, the man-ape, turned and headed back into the swamp. A chorus of hoot owls soothed my jittery nerves.

I shouted, "Will you come back to see me, Bigfoot?"

Off in the distance, I heard his faint but distinctive reply. "Abaluuuubyyyyy."

I stared at Bigfoot's picture on the digital camera. Because of Bigfoot's friendship with Dad, and now with me, I no longer felt alone and afraid. When school starts this fall, maybe I won't be thought of as cool, or popular, but I know my Dad would have been proud of this Gold Star kid.

# BIGFOOT LORE*

- Bigfoot, commonly referred to as Sasquatch, is said to be an ape-like creature inhabiting the forests of North America.

- Bigfoot is believed to be 8-10 ft tall, with reddish-brown hair all over his body and face, and very strong.

- It is also believed Bigfoot has a very bad smell and eats about 60 lbs of food a day.

- Apparently, Bigfoot has very large feet. This helps him walk in harsh environments such as deep snow. Plaster castings of his huge footprints have been made by believers of the man-ape.

- Bigfoot has become an icon within popular culture. Folklorists trace the phenomenon of Bigfoot to sources including the cultures of indigenous people across the continent, the European wild man figure, and folk tales among loggers, miners, trappers, and prospectors.

- Within Canadian and American folklore, "evidence" of the existence of Bigfoot includes numerous anecdotal and visual observations, as well as disputed video and audio recordings, photographs, and casts of large footprints. Most scientists have discounted the existence of Bigfoot, considering its popularity to be the result of a combination of folk tales, misidentification, and hoaxes, rather than a real, living animal.

- The only state in America that hasn't had a Bigfoot sighting is Hawaii.

*from Wikipedia, the free encyclopedia

# MEET THE AUTHOR

## Shelley Anne Richter

Shelley Anne Richter is a professional speaker, author, and storyteller. She was creative story editor for Donna Douglas, an original cast member of "The Beverly Hillbillies."

Shelley is determined to preserve the past, compose literary narratives of the present, and create an imaginative body of work on times yet to come. Her target audiences are precocious children, down-to-earth teens, and wise elders.

CPSIA information can be obtained
at www.ICGtesting.com
Printed in the USA
LVHW080031120122
708313LV00002BA/71